Nan's Rabbit

Nan's Rabbit

Mary Bromilow

illustrations by Alexa Rutherford

ARGYLL ✤ PUBLISHING

© Mary Bromilow 2013

© illustrations Alexa Rutherford 2013

First published by
Argyll Publishing
Glendaruel
Argyll PA22 3AE

The right of Mary Bromilow to be
identified as the author of the work has
been asserted by her in accordance with
the Copyright Designs Act 1988.

**British Library Cataloguing in
Publication Data.
A Catalogue record for this book is
available from the British Library.**

ISBN 978 1 908931 24 5

Printing: Bell & Bain Ltd, Glasgow

for Ethan and Brynn
Mary Bromilow

for Michael
Alexa Rutherford

IT WAS cool where Nan stood, in the barn. But outside, in the yard, it was hot. Nell, the old collie dog, was sleeping in the shade by the barn door.

Everything was quiet.

Nan leaned against the cold stone wall. She was watching the swallows flying to their nests under the beams. They were feeding their babies. She could only see the babies' bright, wide-open beaks, because she wasn't very tall. But she loved watching them.

In the afternoons during the holidays there wasn't much to do. She just got in Mum's way if she stayed in the house.

People thought there was plenty to do on a farm. But when you were eight years old and had nobody to play with, it was different.

The farm didn't belong to Nan's father. He only worked there. She was always being told "don't go in there" or "don't touch that."

She wished she had a pony or a dog of her own to play with. But there was no money to spare. And the dogs were kept for working on the farm, and were too tired to play.

Still, Nan loved animals and birds. Playing on the farm, even on her own, was far better than the streets or play parks.

Nan shifted from one foot to the other as quietly as she could. If she stood really still the birds didn't notice her.

There was a soft thump behind her.

It made Nan jump and she turned round quickly.

Snuggles, the farm cat, had jumped in through the open window. She was carrying something. She put it down as Nan stepped forward.

Snuggles sat back, settled down, and waited.

The small brown bundle she had brought in stirred and hopped forward. It was a baby rabbit.

Snuggles waited until it had hopped a little way. Then she pounced, growling softly. After a minute she let go. The baby rabbit hopped forward again.

"Snuggles! You horrible cruel cat!" Nan raced forward and shooed. Snuggles only glared at her.

"You're NOT going to kill it!" said Nan. She picked up the soft warm bundle.

Snuggles meowed and followed Nan to the door. But Nan pushed the cat back with her foot and shut the barn door in her face.

"You poor wee thing," she said softly, hugging the baby rabbit to her chest.

"I'll take you back to the hill, where you'll be safe."

She could feel the rabbit's heart beating against her hand as she walked along.

Nan opened the hill gate with her other hand. She had to hold it with her foot while she edged round and fastened it.

The rabbit lay very still. She carried it carefully to the nearest rabbit hole she could find. It was in the hillside, not very far from the gate.

Gently she laid the rabbit down on the soft dry soil at the opening of the hole, and stepped back.

It didn't move.

"Go on, you're all right now," said Nan. But the rabbit lay where she had put it, completely still.

Nan stepped back slowly till she was at the dry stone dyke. Then she sat down to watch. She had one eye on the farm track, in case Snuggles came back. But she kept watching the rabbit.

Still it didn't move.

Nan waited.

She saw her father come down the hill with his dogs. She watched him as he went through the gate. It was nearly tea time.

The rabbit still hadn't moved when Nan heard her mother shouting "Nan! Come and get your tea!"

Nan got up and looked at the rabbit. It might have been dead. Somehow she was sure it wasn't. She began to walk down the path to the farm. There was no sign of Snuggles.

When Nan went into the kitchen, her Mum and Dad were at the table.

Her mother laid a plate in front of Nan, and reached for the teapot. "What took you so long?" she asked.

"I was watching a baby rabbit," said Nan. "Snuggles had caught it and I took it from her. I put it back at its hole on the hill."

"Is it still there?" asked her mother.

"It's still lying outside the hole," Nan said. She ate her tea of egg and chips as fast as she could. "I'll need to get back, in case Snuggles finds it again."

"Ye needna bother," said her father. "It'll die, if a fox doesna get it first."

Nan swallowed her last mouthful of tea. She jumped to her feet. "It won't die," she shouted. "I'm going now!"

She ran fast to get to the rabbit hole. The rabbit was still there, exactly as she had left it. She leaned down and looked. One ear twitched, and by the tiny movement of its side, Nan could see its heart beating.

It was alive.

"I hope it gets better before it gets dark," thought Nan. She was thinking about foxes and owls. They could come along at dusk, and would think a baby rabbit was a perfect meal.

"No!" thought Nan, but she knew her mother wouldn't allow her to sit up on the hill till late.

The sun was beginning to go down. Nan had her back to it, but she knew the time by the lengthening shadows. Suddenly she saw a movement at the rabbit hole. She sat up excitedly to watch.

First the ears flickered. The flattened furry bundle became a rabbit shape again. It sat quite still for a moment. Then it moved forward – almost a hop.

"Nan, come and help us shift the calves." It was her mother calling, and Nan jumped.

The rabbit had heard her too. It sat completely still again.

Nan waited. She was scared to move in case she frightened it again.

Then her father shouted, "Nan! Come on!"

Nan trembled. Slowly and quietly she edged her way along the dyke, and climbed over and ran down the path to the farm.

Just at the bottom of the path she met Snuggles going up.

"Oh Snuggles! Trust you to come right now!"

Nan picked up the cat, who meowed loudly and began to struggle.

Nan was badly scratched, but she held on to the twisting, wriggling cat. Finally she arrived in the byre beside her parents.

Her hands and arms were bleeding from the scratches. Snuggles was wailing loudly, but at least Nan knew that her rabbit was safe.

"Put that cat down and come on, we havena got all night." Nan's father unfastened the door of the calf pen as he spoke. "Ye're sittin' up there for nothing. The rabbit'll be dead. And leave the cat alone."

Nan started to cry. "It's NOT dead!" she sobbed.

The calves were out now. They wobbled about the byre with stiff, straight legs. They had been in the pen since they were born, and they were scared.

Snuggles was sitting on a stall, her tail waving.

At a sign from her father Nan opened the byre door. The calves came out, rushing a few steps then stopping and bumping into one another. They were snorting and blowing at this big green world they'd never seen before.

Nan's father thumped his stick on the ground behind them. They all rushed forward again, bellowing and coughing. Sometimes, one would shoot off to one side or the other and had to be brought back.

It seemed to take forever to get to the field gate. The calves rushed through it, leaping into the air and galloping off.

As soon as they were safely in the field, Nan turned to go back up the hill.

"Where're ye goin' now? It's near bed time and ye need to help your mother shut the hens in." Her father sounded angry, and Nan stopped. She looked pleadingly at her mother.

"Let the lassie go." Her mother sounded tired.

"But you've not to be long now, or I'll come and get you."

Nan didn't wait. She ran up the path as fast as she could. She climbed the dyke and tiptoed along until she was near the rabbit hole.

She looked up. There was no rabbit there! No rabbit!

He's got better and gone into the hole. Surely nothing could have happened to him. Nan got down on her hands and knees.

Nan crept along to the opening of the burrow. It was dark at the mouth of the hole. She lay on her stomach and peered in.

And there, just inside, sat a baby rabbit. He was curled up, and his eyes were closed, but he was alive.

"He IS my rabbit!" thought Nan happily. She could see the earth sticking to his side where she had laid him down. What a relief. She wanted to laugh, or cry, or both.

She started to back away, still on her hands and knees. Her knee came down on an old, dry twig. It cracked like a gunshot.

Nan jumped and rubbed her knee, watching the hole.

Her rabbit opened his eyes and sat up. He pricked his ears. With a flash of his little white tail, he vanished into the darkness of the burrow.

"I only hope I picked the right hole," thought Nan. "If I didn't, a rabbit family will have an unexpected visitor!"

As she skipped back down the path, the swallows were making their last swooping calls to feed their babies. It was almost dark.

Her mother was at the door to look for her. Nan was happy. She had saved her rabbit.